Bouncy
and
Cal's Big Show

Brenda Jones

Jim "🏀" Jones

This book is dedicated to all the wonderful teachers we both had growing up in Avon Lake, OH. They challenged us to become our best and help us both find our passion to excel. Thank you to the many teachers like Mrs. Kantor, Mrs. Dematte, Mr. Briggs, Mrs. Reimueller, Mr. Godlewski, Mrs. Schuster, Mr. Stubner, and Mrs. Day.

BOUNCY AND CAL'S BIG SHOW
Copyright © 2021 by Jim and Brenda Jones
Published by Jim Jones Enterprises LLC, Avon Lake, OH

For information regarding permissions email: Jim@JimBasketballJones.com or visit JimBasketballJones.com

Paperback ISBN: 978-1-7350356-6-6
Hardback ISBN: 978-1-7350356-7-3

First Edition: June 2021

Bouncy

and
Cal's Big Show

Jim and Brenda Jones

Cal burst through the front door. With
Bouncy the Basketball tucked tightly under
his arm, he headed for the fridge.

Cal's mom shook her head. "No snacks right now,
dinner's almost ready. How was Talent Show practice?"

Cal rolled his eyes. "Bouncy and I can't get our routine together. We're gonna flop!"

Bouncy nudged Cal. The word 'flop' always reminded him that he was a basketball that couldn't bounce.

"Sorry, Bouncy," Cal said.

During dinner Cal moaned about how hard it was to learn new tricks. His mom nodded thoughtfully. After dinner she brought Cal a piece of chocolate cake.

Cal *loved* cake! But when he tried to poke his fork into it, it fell off the table and bounced! Bouncy giggled.

Cal picked up the piece of cake and squished it. When he let go, it sprang back into its cake shape.

"What *is* this?"

Mom smiled. "It's made of foam. Remember when I gave you the stuffed Yeti? He was a reminder that you just hadn't learned something, YET. Well, the power behind the YET is a Piece of Cake!"

Cal scratched his head. "What does fake cake have to do with Yeti?"

Bouncy wiggled with excitement. He *loved* a good mystery.

Mom explained, "A piece of cake is the power *behind* the Yet. You haven't learned it, yet, but you can learn if you break it into little pieces. Then you take it one piece at a time, just like a piece of cake."

Cal still looked confused.

Mom added, "If you eat a whole cake all at once you get a belly ache, right?"

"Uh, yeah." Cal didn't like to think about how rotten he felt the time he ate a whole cake. He was so sick he didn't even get into trouble.

Mom smiled. "It's much better to eat a cake one piece at a time. Take the piece of cake with you when you practice. It will help you just like Yeti did.

"And I'll bake you a real chocolate cake so you can have some after the talent show."

For the next week, Cal and Bouncy practiced and practiced. When they couldn't do a trick, Bouncy said, "Let's break it into little pieces, just like a piece of cake!"

Cal did, and it worked. Somehow, knowing the power behind the Yet helped him relax and learn the trick one piece at a time.

Bouncy *loved* learning tricks like a piece of cake — you could even say he was having a ball!

On the day of the Talent Show, Bouncy showed the piece of cake to Yeti and Speedy. He said, "I don't think we could have learned the new tricks without it!"

"Can you help me get the piece of cake into Cal's backpack so we'll have it for tonight?"

Yeti picked up the piece of cake and squeezed it. Then he let go and laughed as it sprang out of his fur paws. He stuffed the piece of cake into the top of Cal's backpack. He had to leave the pack open because he couldn't work the zipper with his furry paws.

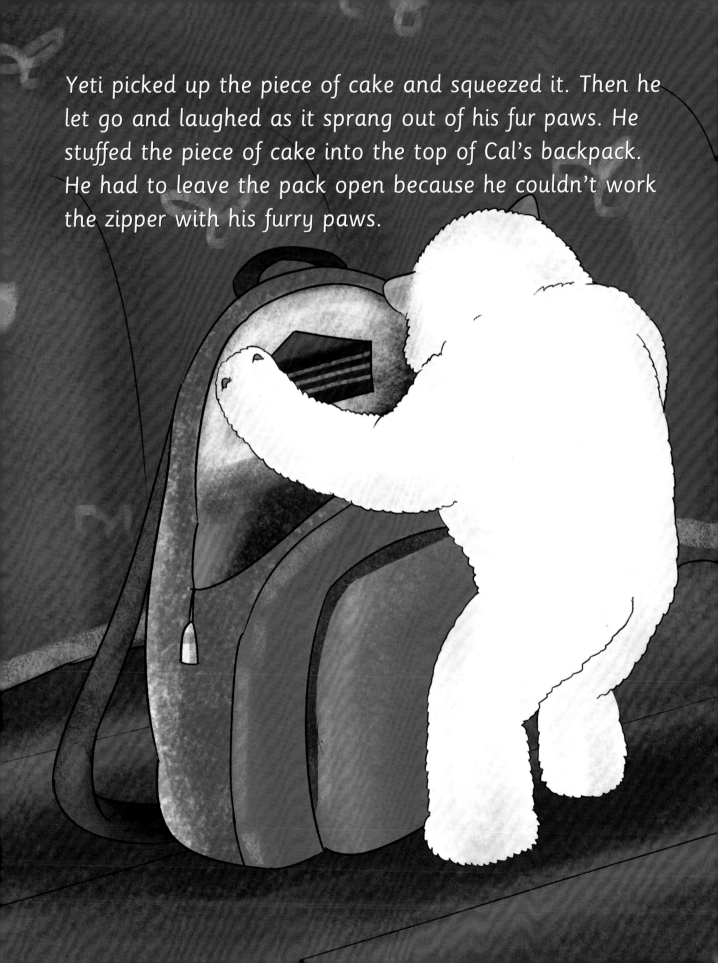

Just then, Cal ran into the room and yelled, "Bouncy, it's SHOW time! Are you ready to go?"

Bouncy grinned with confidence. "I'm ready to roll!"

Cal scooped up Bouncy and threw his backpack over his shoulder. As he ran out of the room, the piece of cake bounced out of his pack and onto the floor.

Speedy revved his engine
as Yeti jumped on.

Yeti grabbed the piece of
cake and...

zoooom!
They were off!

They **flew** down the staircase,

smashed through the doggy door

and **raced** down the front steps to the sidewalk.

Yeti held on tight as Speedy made
a sharp right turn.

Eeeeeek!

Speedy went up on two wheels and they almost
flipped over. Yeti was afraid he might lose his lunch,
but he held on tightly to the piece of cake!

The sidewalk ended with a tall curb and Yeti held his breath as Speedy sailed over it and made a perfect landing.

"Way to go, Speedy!" Yeti shouted. "All that ramp jumping practice just paid off!"

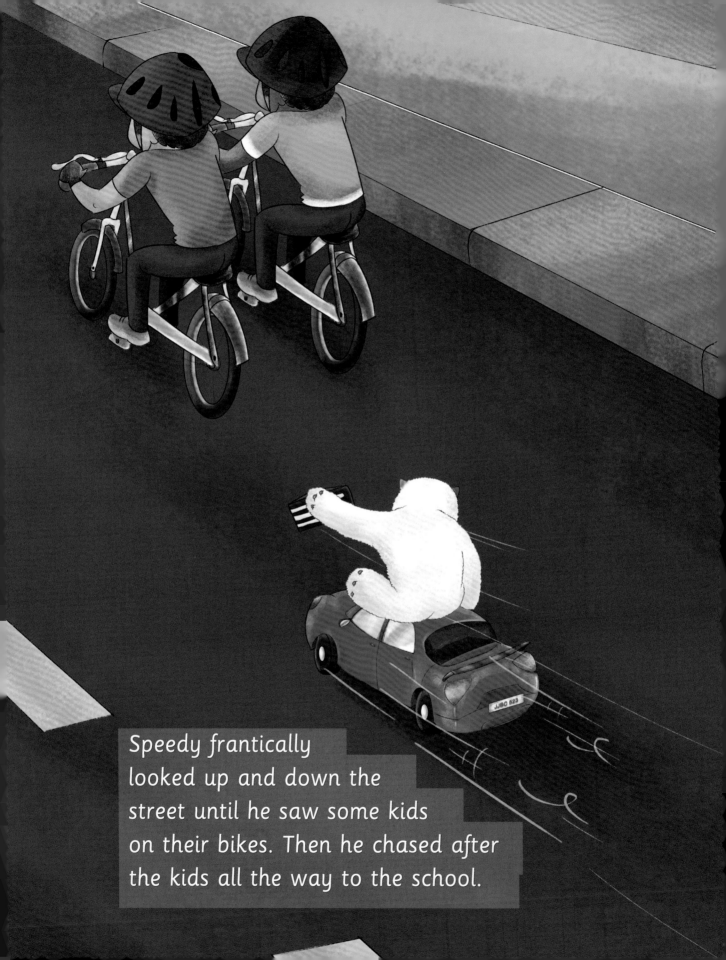

Speedy frantically looked up and down the street until he saw some kids on their bikes. Then he chased after the kids all the way to the school.

Screech! Speedy came to a stop at the school parking lot. "Yeti, it's your turn! How do we get in?!! How do we find Cal and Bouncy?!!"

Yeti said, "I don't know, YET, but I'll figure it out!"

Yeti watched where the kids were going.

"That way! The back door is open!"

Speedy zoomed through the door and into the backstage area where kids were getting ready for the show.

Yeti pointed.
"Over there!
On the far side!
Go, Speedy, go!"

Speedy tried to reach Cal, but he had to zip between the feet of dozens of kids. When they finally got close, Speedy yelled, "Yeti! Throw the piece of cake!"

Yeti flung the piece of cake just as Speedy made a sharp left to avoid running into a boy.

Speedy spun out as the piece of cake bounced and rolled right into Cal's feet.

Cal picked up the piece of cake and looked around until he saw Yeti and Speedy.

Speedy flashed his lights and Cal flashed a huge grin. He shoved the piece of cake into his pocket.

Driving home after the show, Cal talked on and on about what fun he had doing tricks with Bouncy and how the other kids loved their act.

Mom looked at Cal and said, "I'm proud of you, son! You worked hard and you didn't quit even when things got tough!"

Cal smiled. "It was a piece of cake...

Cake!

Did you bake the cake?!!"

Bouncy and Friends Book Series

All books available at www.JimBasketballJones.com/shop

The first book in the series is *Bouncy: The Basketball That Couldn't Bounce*. Bouncy is an adorable and lovable basketball that feels hopeless and sad when he finds out he can't bounce. A boy named Cal finds Bouncy and says to him, "You are the one and only you. I'll help you find what you can do."

This picture book helps children realize that they are unique and special.

In the second book, Bouncy and The Power of Yet, Bouncy and Yeti help a remote control car, Speedy, overcome his fears about jumping over a ramp. "My box said I jump ramps, but I'm too scared! What if I crash? What if my wheels come off and everybody laughs at me?!!" Speedy explains. Yeti helps Speedy realize he just doesn't know how to jump the ramp YET, but he can learn.

This picture book helps children realize they can learn new things and it's okay to make mistakes. You just don't know it yet. You can get your own Yeti stuffed animal at:

www.JimBasketballJones.com/shop.

In the third book in the series, Bouncy and Cal's Big Show, Cal and Bouncy are struggling to create a fun basketball routine for the school Talent Show. Cal's mom gives them a secret tip that makes learning the new routine a "piece of cake." It works, but then the night of the BIG SHOW they lose the piece of cake. Speedy and Yeti have to come to the rescue and get the piece of cake to the school before the Talent Show.

In this fun and adventuresome picture book children discover a secret tip on how to make learning a "piece of cake."

About the Authors

Jim "Basketball" Jones, MBA is a National Youth Motivational Speaker and Author with over 20 years as a professional school assembly speaker. With over 8,000 school assemblies performed, Jim is a leader in the school assembly and character education field.

Book Jim for an **Author Visit** or **School Assembly** for your school. Find out how to schedule Jim at:
www.JimBasketballJones.com.
You can follow Jim on
Facebook @JimBasketballJones and
Twitter @JimBballJones

Brenda Jones, M. Ed. is an award winning educator (Franklin B Walters Award Recipient) with over 25 years of teaching experience. She loves helping kids learn how to break down their learning into smaller pieces. She is the mother to four wonderful children, two very furry puppies and is an Ace Fitness Instructor. She credits her passion for teaching to her parents who were both elite educators. You can follow Brenda on Twitter @KdngDisneyJones